Donkey's Dreadful Day

written and illustrated by
Irina Hale

A Margaret K. McElderry Book

Atheneum   1982   New York

jp

64407

By the same author: **Chocolate Mouse and Sugar Pig and How They Ran Away to Escape Being Eaten**

Library of Congress catalog card number 81-10773   ISBN 0-689-50221-4   Copyright © 1982 by Irina Hale   All rights reserved.   First Edition

Printed in Hong Kong by South China Printing Co.

A lovely smell of stew drifted
out of the cook's tent in the circus.
Donkey thought:
"How I wish *I* could be cook!
I would eat carrots all day long,
And there would always be more!"

Cook looked at Donkey and said:

"Do you want to be cook?

All right, come on!

Here is a list of all the different foods.

You must give steaks to the lions,

and fish to the sea lions,

a bone to the little dog . . .

and cauliflower to Hippo Rosie.

The clowns eat spaghetti.

The crocodiles must have . . ."

But Donkey was too excited to listen any longer.

So now Donkey *was* cook.
He stirred the bears' mush,
which was boiling over, and
put salt in the ringmaster's coffee.
Something was burning—
Was it the lions' beefsteaks?

"Hurry, Cook!
The ringmaster wants his coffee,
the fire-eater wants his sausages
and ice cream!"
Donkey held the list
upside down
and tried to remember . . .

With a lot of helpers
he started to take the food around.
But Donkey couldn't quite remember
what he was to feed each animal.

"Now let me see.

Wasn't it steaks for the sea lions?" he asked himself.

The real lions
got live, slithery fish.
They growled.
"We'd rather eat up the cook instead . . ."

"Here's a nice big cauliflower,
a surprise for a hungry little dog . . ." Donkey said
as he rushed on.

Hippo Rosie was next.
For her there was a tiny dog bone.
Where was the lovely cauliflower she always had?

The clowns were so hungry for their spaghetti,
they couldn't even wait to take off their false noses.

But when the lid came off the dish . . .
it was a pile of elephants' hay!

The elephants got the spaghetti instead.
"It's nice," they said,
"but we're still hungry!"

Donkey put so much
pepper on it that . . .

a big elephant
sneezed him right out of the tent!

The camels didn't look very pleased
with their boiled eggs.
Cactus plants would have tasted better.

The poor lady acrobat got
the cactus instead.
Donkey brought a plant
he had found
on a caravan windowsill.

"Does a crocodile like ice cream?" Donkey wondered.
"Here, eat it fast," he said. "It's melting!"
But the crocodiles seemed to prefer
the fire-eater's sausages!

"Oh, Mr. Fire-Eater!" Donkey said,
"I'm sure you will enjoy
some lighted matches
for your supper, won't you?"
But the fire-eater shouted,
"I WANT MY SAUSAGES!"
"Oh dear . . ." said Donkey.

"And is that my ice cream
under that lid?" said Mr. Fire-Eater hopefully.
But it wasn't at all.
Some playful frogs had hidden there!

The ringmaster saw Monkey coming
with a huge soup tureen.
"Is that soup?" he said and he took a spoonful.
"Ooh, delicious!"
The monkey didn't tell him that
it was really the bears' mush!

By the time Donkey got to the bears,
he had only the ringmaster's
coffee to give them.
"What fun to juggle with
cups and saucers!" said the bears.

Before long, a lot of cross and hungry animals
arrived at the cook's tent.
The ringmaster had decided to inspect the kitchen, too.
He wanted more bears' mush,
but the bears had got there first!

Luckily the real cook had come back
and was busy at work!

Donkey crept out
at the back of the tent.
"One day of being cook
is enough for me!" he said.

Before long, everyone had found
their proper food
and they were all happy again.

There was just one biscuit left
for the helpers to share
between them.
They felt *very* sad.

Back in the stables,
Donkey sighed.
"This is my first bit of carrot all day!
Maybe I should be careful
what I want to be, next time . . ."
But soon he was dreaming
of being someone really exciting
—a cowboy-donkey, perhaps?
You can never stop Donkey
from being a donkey,
can you?

jP   Hale,

          Donkey's dreadful
          day

                  64407

DATE			

1986